This book is dedicated to my husband, thank you for finding and bringing home the best gift ever, one that makes us smile daily. X

PREFACE

Someone was watching me, who was it? Then I saw him, I had to bring him home..............

The Cop and the Cat by Julie Chapman

Contents

Chapter 1 – Another day begins ...

Another day begins and the routine starts all over again.

I had joined the Police force in 2003 and here we are, October 2016 and I'm still going. Like all jobs there are good days and bad days. Today was a day when I was definitely thinking there has to be more to life than this!

We had a good life.

I'd been married to Ju since 1998, we had met when we were 23. We socialised .... a lot! We took holidays to wonderful places, and I suppose I had to work to pay for it all. We hadn't had any children and so had filled our lives with animals. We had Roger the Rabbit and Harry the cat, however since they had both passed away in 2007 we'd stuck to guinea pigs.

So, today started like any other day.
Alarm, shower, shave, cuppa and off to work.
I arrived at work at the 7.45 a.m. nothing out of
the ordinary there, but today something felt
different. Weird. I honestly felt like someone
was watching me. I looked around the street,
up and down, but couldn't see anyone – Oh
well, I must be imaging things.

Day after day I arrived at the same time and
each day I felt like someone was watching me, it
was starting to bug me.
Who was it?
I scoured the street for the person responsible,
but no one to be seen.
This has been happening for a couple of weeks
now.

The day was much the same and again the
minutes ticked by and home time was upon us.
I left the station and walked across the road to
the car. What was that on my roof?

I could see a shape lying there in the sunshine.
An orange colour. Wow! It was a cat, basking
in the late autumn sunshine, a kindred spirit I
thought.
I adore the sun, always have done, if I can't seek
out the actual sun then the local sunbed shop is
the place to be, hence when Ju and I met my
nick name was 'Tan Man'.

I approached the car and the cat looked up.
Our eyes met. Huge green eyes. He just lay
there looking at me looking at him. As I got
closer he jumped off and ran away. Oh cute cat,
I thought. I wondered briefly if it was him
who'd been watching me? Then I drove home
and didn't think any more of it.

The same routine continued day after day,
however, he got more and more brave and
would stay put as I approached. I would walk
across the road and say "come on mate, off you
get", and he would look at me again with his

huge green eyes and then jump off, making a little squeaking noise as he did.

One day I popped home to collect my lunch and Ju was chopping up some leftover steak for the local visiting cat, we called him Puss-Puss, a suitable name for a cat who's name you don't know, we thought.

Puss-Puss would visit daily for treats and crunchies. He was such a handsome cat. I missed having a cat about the house – as they say a cat makes a house a home!

I asked Ju if I could have some of the food and she looked at me with a strange look. I explained that it wasn't for me, and began to tell her about this little ginger cat that was obviously hungry as he was so thin. She immediately gave me that 'don't even think about it look' before passing me a little bag of chopped up steak.

I returned to work and parked the car; I looked all around but couldn't see him. I shouted "c'mon mate", but no sign of him. Ahh what a shame, I didn't want the steak to go to waste – so OK what next?

Where was he? I know, I will try the internationally renowned pussy cat call (I know this because I have tried it when I have been abroad). I made the noise and yes it worked. His little ginger head popped up from over the road under a bush in someone's garden. I made the noise again and called him. He came running across the road. He looked at me with those huge eyes and rubbed around my legs purring. I could tell that we were most definitely friends.

I gave him the steak; he wolfed it down, all the time looking around for predators who may want to steal his food.

Our first meal together.

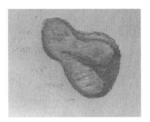

He didn't look well my new little mate. He had a cut on his face, his fur was very sparse and he was so very thin. I was starting to wonder if he must be a stray. I had been asking around the neighbourhood to see if anyone owned him. The local residents had told me that he had been around for about five weeks but no one knew who he belonged to.

Chapter 2 – I loved Fridays!

It was Friday. YAY, I loved Fridays!
Relaxing evening, a few beers and a curry with
Ju. I left work and approached my car feeling
disappointed that the little ginger cat wasn't
around today. It was cold and rainy so
hopefully he was somewhere warm.

I pulled out and started to drive up the road,
the car was roaring abnormally and then clatter,
clatter, clunk, BANG! What had just happened?
Then I realised - the exhaust had fallen off.
Drat! I was stuck. Luckily a friend offered me a
lift home so Friday could commence after-all.

As we drove home, I was thinking about him,
that poor little ginger cat, with his sore face and
hardly any fur, and worrying that I wouldn't be
around over the weekend. I hope he will be OK.

He really played on my mind, and that's when I decided! Right! I needed to put my plan into place. My mission would be to convince Ju that she does need a cat in her life!

I talked about him constantly all over the weekend. By Sunday evening she clearly felt like killing me. Ju was adamant that we were not having another cat. I did understand that after we lost Harry, we were devastated. She didn't want to go through that again and so I knew why she was saying it. But was now the right time?

Monday morning came round, all too soon. I hadn't done anything about my car over the weekend so Ju said she would drop me off at work.

We drove to the station and she was just about to pull into a parking space outside the station, which was littered with leaves, and then she stopped suddenly.

"What are you doing", I asked as she had slammed the brakes on quite suddenly.

She just looked at me and said "LOOK" - She had spotted him! He was sat there hunched up on a bed of autumn leaves, blending in due to his colouring. I jumped out of the car and went to give him some love and see if he was OK, but unfortunately Ju had to leave as there was traffic behind her. I gave my little mate a stroke and he looked into my eyes "not long now mate, hang on in there" I said. The plan had worked – Ju had seen him and I had seen that look in her eyes as she drove off!

I called her later on that day and the first thing she said was "OK, we need to have that cat, he's not well". I knew it! My cunning plan had definitely worked! The cat had played his part perfectly too. Right place right time, my little ginger friend.

Ju was coming to pick me up that evening and we set about working out how to get him. I contacted my Dad and asked him if he had a cat basket. He said no, but he would get one for us. He went off, a man on a mission.

When Ju arrived she had the basket that my Dad had borrowed. We both looked at each other......... "Where on earth did Dad get that from?", I asked and she laughed.
Seriously, we'd be lucky to get a guinea pig in it, it was that tiny. She had also brought some chicken with her to tempt him.

Immediately the little ginger cat came over to see us. Ju could see how poorly he was. She tried to feed him the chicken, however, although interested he didn't eat much of it.

We tried to get him into the basket.
Unfortunately our plan failed! Not only was he a stubborn little chap, he refused to get into the basket, no way. It was far too small.

We weren't to be defeated; we just needed a little extra help so on the way home I called the RSPCA. I explained who I was and I played the Policeman card to add more weight to the story. I also explained that he was so poorly and now had a huge lump on the side of his face.

The next day the RSPCA called me back and said that if I could catch him and take him to the local vets on their behalf they would take it from there. So my colleague and I found a large cardboard box, caught him and put him in it. Simple as that, we thought! We sealed the lid and put it in the car and off I went, to get this little puss to safety.
Except not!

He had different ideas, summoned all his strength and forced his head out of the box. I was driving up the street with a large cardboard box on the seat and a little ginger head poking out the top. He wasn't stopping there and he struggled until he ended up on the dashboard writhing around.

Now, I'm a Police Officer ………… What must this have looked like to the passing public? I couldn't carry on driving with him there on the dash of the car. I had no choice but to pull over and let him out. He ran off. "Drat", had I blown it. Had I scared him so that he'd be gone for good? I parked up and got out of the car and started to walk back to the station, and there he was, those big eyes looking up at me! He immediately started to rub around my legs and purr.

OK, so Plan A and Plan B had now failed. He was sick and wasn't getting any better.

Time to put Plan C into operation. I called the RSPCA again and explained my failure. They agreed to come and collect him the next day.

So the next day they called me to say they had managed to get him. "He's a feisty little thing isn't he", said the lady. He certainly was.

We were so relieved he was finally safe. Whatever happened now, at least he was in a safe place and able to get the medical attention he needed.

Between Ju and me we called the RSPCA centre daily, sometimes more than once, to check on his progress. I think they got a little fed up with us as one lady told Ju off, telling her that only one of us should call – once a day. We couldn't help it, we cared about him already – Ju had only met him once, but he had got to her. As for me, I was already in love.

The RSPCA confirmed that once he was well we could adopt him and we were so excited, but a little apprehensive too as we hadn't had a cat for 9 ½ years. He had chosen me though, we were both really sure of that.

He stayed with the RSPCA for a week. He had an operation on an abscess on his face; he also had a polyp removed from his ear, oh yes and his bits removed – OUCH.

Chapter 3 – A week later...

A week later Ju called and was given the news that he could come home. We were so excited. I was on shift so Ju went to collect him, after stopping off at the shops to stock up on all things cat related. Any excuse to shop.

After signing all the official adoption papers they were free to go. He was strapped into the front seat (in his new appropriately sized basket, obviously) and off they set – homeward bound.

I called later on that day to check that they had made it home safely and to see how he was settling in. Ju said that he had just peeped out of the basket, so she left him to it and went to set up his litter tray and bowls etc. When she retuned to the living room the basket was empty and there was no sign of him. Then his head popped up over the arm of the sofa.

His Auntie Karen had been to see him and Ju told me how she had gone to stroke him and he had lashed her one! Yep he certainly was a feisty little thing – and we were going to find out just how much!

He had had a wee in his litter tray (which was good as my wife would have killed me if he had peed on the carpet), and had had something to eat.

I arrived home and peeped though the window. He was sat on the sofa. My large frame and large coat must have frightened him because he ran and hid behind the sofa, staying there for ages. I was sad, after everything I had done to save him, and hurt that he was scared of me. He eventually came out and realised that I wasn't going to hurt him and rubbed around my legs purring.

More friends and relatives came to see him, he watched them with curiosity from under the dining table. He did venture off for a little love with his Auntie Jodie and then he went straight back under the table. He stayed there for two days only coming out to eat and use his litter tray. He eventually started to gain his confidence and settled in, I think he knew that this was his forever home.

Chapter 4 - Bob

After a few more weeks of vets visits (which he hated), and rest and recuperation he was as right as rain. His hair grew back, his face healed up and he began to gain weight. He started to play with the numerous toys he now had, and his character started to really start to show.

He was no longer an ugly duckling, he was a handsome swan.

He was now allowed out. We waited nervously for him to return, which thankfully he did. He could be trusted. Well kind of…….

One day we opened the front door and he darted across the road straight up the large tree opposite, right to the top. Ju was screaming "call the fire brigade, call the fire brigade", I was like "OMG, OMG", then he manoeuvred his little body around and shimmied down the tree backwards – clever little boy. This became a regular occurrence, especially if he didn't want to come in, he would dart across the road, right up the tree, his eyes huge green eyes alive with naughtiness.

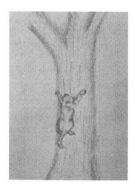

"He chose me, he decided he wanted to be with me and he made it happen"

We called him Bob.

Printed in Great Britain
by Amazon